Poptropica®

LUNAR COLONY

POPTROPICA

Published by the Penguin Group

Penguin Group (USA) Inc., 375 Hudson Street, New York, New York 10014, USA

USA | Canada | UK | Ireland | Australia | New Zealand | India | South Africa | China
Penguin Books Ltd, Registered Offices: 80 Strand, London WC2R 0RL, England

For more information about the Penguin Group visit penguin.com

ISBN 978-0-448-46354-4   10 9 8 7 6 5 4 3 2 1

LUNAR C🌑LONY

WITHDRAWN

adapted by Patrick Kinney
cover illustrated by Angel Rodriguez
illustrated by Abraham Evensen Tena

Poptropica
An Imprint of Penguin Group (USA) Inc.

Chapter One

Salerno

The words flashed brightly across the computer monitor, but Commander Rachel Salerno was too busy to notice. Instead, she sat hunched over her workstation, poring over the mountain of notes, maps, and drawings that littered her desk.

"Where are you, Number Four?" she mumbled to herself. As the only astronaut remaining on the moon, she talked to herself a lot these days. True, the lunar facility felt quiet and lonely without the chatter of the other astronauts who had once lived and worked with Salerno, but at least there weren't any distractions now, especially when she was so close to finding what she was looking for.

"I know you're out there," she said, her brow

furrowed. Suddenly, she noticed something in one of the pictures, a detail she'd missed until now. Barely able to contain her excitement, she grabbed a page of notes from the pile of papers. Looking back and forth between her notes and the picture, she let out a gasp.

"Of course! If my calculations are correct, then Number Four must be located in the Northeast Sector! But where?" she asked, her voice echoing down the empty hall of the barracks.

As she pondered this question, she sat back in her chair and, for the first time, noticed the blinking words on the computer monitor. With a click of the mouse, she retrieved the message from her in-box. As she read, her sparkling eyes grew dark.

COMMANDER SALERNO, AGAIN AND AGAIN YOU HAVE DISOBEYED MY ORDERS. YOUR INSISTENCE ON IGNORING YOUR DUTIES AND CONTINUING THIS SILLY QUEST OF YOURS IS SIMPLY UNACCEPTABLE. AS I'VE SAID BEFORE, THIS IS NO TIME TO BE SEARCHING FOR LITTLE GREEN MEN. I AM SENDING SOMEONE TO RELIEVE YOU AND BRING YOU BACK TO EARTH. YOU

ARE ADVISED TO GATHER YOUR BELONGINGS AND
PREPARE FOR YOUR RETURN HOME.

-ROGER MCNABB, DIRECTOR OF THE POPTROPICA
ACADEMY OF SPACE EXPLORATION

"So, McNabb's sending someone to get me, is he? I'm on a 'silly quest,' am I?" Salerno put her face in her hands, feeling much like a cornered animal. For a moment she sat still, weighing her few options. At last she sat up straight and looked defiantly at the message on the computer screen, as though she was looking at McNabb himself. "No, McNabb, you can't stop me now, not when I'm so close to finding Number Four!"

And with this, she left her workstation and began making preparations for her escape.

Chapter Two

Father and Son

Back on Earth, Glen Johns struggled to keep up with his father as they walked across the parking lot toward Cape Carpenter. Mr. Johns could barely keep himself from sprinting to the space center's entrance.

"Gosh, this is exciting, isn't it, Glen?" said Mr. Johns, who was huffing and puffing from the brisk pace. "To think that we're here to see the very last space launch is just amazing!"

Glen didn't say anything. He was tired from the long car ride and feeling a little cranky. Plus, he hadn't really wanted to come to Cape Carpenter in the first place.

"It's not every day you get to be a part of—"

"History. I know, Dad," said Glen. "You already said that, like, ten times in the car."

Mr. Johns chuckled. "Well, it's true. They're

shutting down the space program after this launch." After a pause he added quietly, "It's sad, really, but at least we're here to say good-bye."

Glen heard his father but, again, didn't reply. Instead, he eyed the rocket off in the distance. It looked very small sitting on its launchpad hundreds of yards away. But Glen knew that it was enormous. The first time he and his dad came to watch a launch, he was only four years old. The rocket was the biggest, most exciting thing Glen had ever seen. "Faster, Daddy," Glen had said as they raced across the parking lot, holding hands.

But Glen was thirteen years old now. He no longer needed to hold his father's hand, and he didn't really care about rockets or space travel anymore. Like dinosaurs and superheroes, space was just something he'd outgrown over the years. As he walked, he looked at the excitement on his father's face and wondered how a grown-up could care so much about something so silly.

"Yeah," said Mr. Johns, "it's hard to believe that there will be no more space launches after today. What a shame."

"Dad, if you think the space program is so important, why are they shutting it down?" Glen asked.

The question stung Mr. Johns a bit. He knew that his son was no longer a little boy and that he'd become interested in other things. Still, hearing Glen say "if *you* think it's so important" made him a little sad. He remembered the days when they both thought that space travel was important and looked forward to their special days together at Cape Carpenter. Inside, Mr. Johns had hoped for just one more of those special days.

"Well," replied Mr. Johns, "I guess most people don't care about space travel the way they used to. And since the people aren't interested anymore, the government decided to spend its money on other things."

"Well, maybe the people are right," Glen said. "I mean, what's the point of going into space?"

"To explore!" Mr. Johns replied. "Think back to the days of Christopher Columbus and the other great explorers. What they all had in common was the desire to know what's out there."

Glen frowned and said, "I don't know, Dad, it seems like we've pretty much discovered all there is to find."

Mr. Johns smiled, thinking back to the days when Glen would stay up way past his bedtime, asking question after question about the moon, the stars, and the planets of the galaxy. Back then, the boy was filled with so much wonder, so much curiosity. At last, Mr. Johns said, "Son, the universe is a mighty big place. It seems to me that it'd be a shame if we ever stopped exploring it."

Glen resisted the urge to roll his eyes, but he couldn't stop himself from muttering, "Space travel might have been cool, like, a million years ago, but maybe it's time to accept that things have changed."

Yes, they certainly have, Mr. Johns thought. *And it doesn't look like they'll ever be the way they were.*

Father and son walked the rest of the way in silence, until they reached the entrance to Cape Carpenter.

Chapter Three

Cape Carpenter

"Where is everyone?" said Mr. Johns in astonishment as he passed through the gates to Cape Carpenter's outdoor promenade. In years past, it would have been filled with hundreds, even thousands, of space enthusiasts on launch days. Today, though, there was only a small group of people milling about. The crowd was so small, in fact, that Mr. Johns wondered if he had the day of the launch wrong. He approached a man handing out brochures, assuming he'd have some answers.

"Excuse me, sir," said Mr. Johns, "today is the day of the launch, isn't it?"

"Indeed, it is," replied the man. "And once they wrap up this last little mission, construction will begin on Cosmic Condos."

"Cosmic Condos?"

"That's right," said the man. "All these

buildings you see here will be torn down, and in their place will be the most luxurious, most modern apartment buildings you've ever seen. Here, why don't you take one of these brochures and consider purchasing—"

"No, thanks," said Mr. Johns. "We're just here to watch the launch." As he and Glen walked on, he said, "I can't believe they're replacing all this with condos! It's bad enough that the space program is closing down, but this is a historical landmark. Do they really have to take that away, too?"

Glen was tempted to repeat what he'd already said about changing times, but he saw that his dad was a little shaken and decided to keep quiet.

"Well," Mr. Johns said with a weak laugh, "at least we're here on the right day." Then he saw something that seemed to brighten his spirits. "Glen, look! It's Captain Gordon!"

Sitting at a small table behind a sign that said MEET A REAL ASTRONAUT was a silver-haired man of about eighty years. He was there to sign autographs, but since no one was in line, he killed time with a crossword puzzle.

"Captain Gordon?" Glen asked. "Who's that?"

"Don't you remember?" Mr. Johns replied. "Deke Gordon was once one of the biggest names in space exploration, a real hero! Why, if it wasn't for him, we wouldn't know the first thing about how weightlessness affects hamster behavior! Come on, let's go meet him."

Glen didn't recognize the name, but he followed his father, who was already approaching the man.

"Captain Gordon, this sure is a treat," Mr. Johns said to the retired astronaut.

"Well!" replied Gordon, putting down his puzzle. "It's nice to be remembered by *someone*. You're the first person to actually recognize me. The only other person I talked to just stopped by to ask me if Cape Carpenter still sells those rocket-shaped ice pops."

"Are you kidding?" Mr. Johns said, his hands shaking with excitement. "I idolized you as a kid. I had a poster in my bedroom of you walking on the moon!"

"Yes, those were some great days," Captain Gordon said with a laugh. "But they happened long, long ago, I'm afraid." Pointing at a picture on the table, he added, "It's hard to believe that this man and I are the same person." Glen and Mr. Johns looked at the picture, which showed a much younger Captain Gordon riding on the back of a convertible, as thousands of parade-goers cheered him on.

"I remember that," Mr. Johns said. "That was right after you returned from building the first lunar facility on the moon!"

"You have a good memory," Captain Gordon said, smiling. "Yes, back in those days, people couldn't get enough of space exploration. We astronauts were like rock stars!" Then, his smile fading, he added, "But as you can see, things have changed."

Glen had been listening quietly, but he understood what Captain Gordon meant. Hardly anyone had come to watch the launch, and no one cared about meeting some retired astronaut.

"Captain Gordon," said Mr. Johns, looking to

brighten the mood, "this is my son, Glen. He and I have been to half a dozen space launches."

"It's nice to meet you, Glen," said Captain Gordon. "I'm happy to see that there are some young people who still have an interest in space exploration."

Glen's face reddened. He didn't have the heart to tell Captain Gordon that he wasn't really interested in space anymore, or that he would rather be at home watching television. Instead, he just shook the astronaut's hand.

"Glen," Mr. Johns said, "do you have any questions you'd like to ask Captain Gordon?"

The boy blushed even more. "Uh," he said, looking down at his feet. "*Do* they still sell those rocket-shaped ice pops here?"

Captain Gordon raised his eyebrows in surprise.

"Ha-ha," Mr. Johns laughed. "He's just joking. Captain Gordon, thanks so much for your time. Meeting you was a thrill!"

"The pleasure was mine," the astronaut replied. "I hope your last visit to Cape Carpenter is memorable. Enjoy the launch."

"Ice pops?" Mr. Johns said under his breath as he and Glen moved on. "That's the only thing you could think to ask?"

"I'm sorry, Dad," Glen said, feeling irritated. "I didn't know I was supposed to have a list of prepared questions."

Mr. Johns paused and collected himself. "Yeah, Glen," he said, "you're right. I shouldn't have put you on the spot like that. Hey, we still have about an hour before the launch. How about we grab something to eat and then hit the gift shop?"

Glen wasn't angry anymore, but he felt like he could use a break from his dad. "Uh, if you don't mind, I'd kind of like to walk around on my own for a while."

"Oh," Mr. Johns said, feeling like his plans for a perfect day were going south. "But I thought we were going to hang out together today."

"We have been together, Dad," Glen said. "We spent the car ride together, we'll watch the launch together, and we'll drive home together. But I'm thirteen years old; I'm not a little kid anymore. I just want to be by myself for a little while."

"Um, I guess that's okay," Mr. Johns said a little reluctantly. He'd noticed that Glen reminded him that he was thirteen a lot these days. "Here," he said, handing Glen a few dollars, "take this and let's meet up in the spectator stands in an hour."

"Okay, thanks, Dad," Glen said, taking the money. He began walking away but didn't get very far before he heard his father's voice.

"Glen," Mr. Johns called, "be careful!"

Glen didn't turn to acknowledge that he'd heard his dad. He just walked on, rolling his eyes. *Sheesh,* he thought, *it's just an hour. It's not as though I'm going to the moon.*

Chapter Four

Salerno

"COMMANDER SALERNO, I MUST REMIND YOU THAT YOU HAVE BEEN ORDERED TO REMAIN AT THIS LUNAR FACILITY."

Salerno was pushing aside the stacks of paper on her desk and stuffing a few belongings into a bag. She ignored the robot that was following her around.

Let's see, the commander said to herself. *If I can just find my notebook, I can get out of here.*

"COMMANDER SALERNO, I MUST REMIND YOU—" the robot began again.

"I heard you the first time, Nat," Salerno snapped. She didn't have time for a lecture. "Darn!" she said. "Where is that notebook?"

She gave up her search, figuring she knew everything in her journal by heart anyway. She exited the barracks and started walking down the long corridor leading to the vehicle bay. Rolling right behind her was Nat, the facility's robot. Newcomers often mistook Nat for a fancy trash can. More than once, rookie astronauts had tossed bubble gum wrappers and other trash squarely in his digital face.

"COMMANDER SALERNO," Nat said, "I'M BECOMING CONCERNED. IS IT YOUR PLAN TO LEAVE THE LIVING QUARTERS DESPITE MR. MCNABB'S ORDERS TO REMAIN HERE?"

Salerno could see that it was impossible to ignore the robot. She had to try something else.

"Of course not," she said, looking down at him. "I just need to go to the vehicle bay to get something. But I'm not going anywhere."

"THAT IS A RELIEF TO ME," Nat said, his orange eyes brightening. "I WAS GROWING WORRIED THAT YOU WERE GOING TO FLEE."

"Oh, Nat," Salerno said sweetly, "you worry too much. Of course I'm going to obey orders."

"THAT IS GOOD. AS YOU KNOW, I AM PROGRAMMED TO ENSURE THAT ALL DIRECTIVES ARE FOLLOWED."

"That's why I love you, Nat," Salerno said as

she entered the vehicle bay. "You're always here to keep me on track."

"NOW THAT YOU HAVE ARRIVED AT THE VEHICLE BAY, WHAT ITEM IS IT THAT YOU ARE IN SEARCH OF? PERHAPS I CAN HELP YOU FIND IT," Nat offered.

"No, thanks, Nat," Salerno said, picking up a brick-shaped mechanism from one of the workbenches. "I already found it."

Nat's glowing eyes dimmed, as though he was becoming suspicious. "COMMANDER SALERNO, THAT IS THE LOCATOR DEVICE USED TO TRACK THE SIGNAL EMITTED BY YOUR SUIT. FOR WHAT PURPOSE ARE YOU IN NEED OF THAT OBJECT?"

"Oh, I just need to keep it out of the wrong hands," she said, putting it into her bag.

"COMMANDER SALERNO, IT APPEARS THAT YOU HAVE DECEIVED ME," Nat said. "I SEE BY YOUR ACTIONS THAT YOU ARE PLANNING TO ESCAPE FROM THIS FACILITY."

"You are a bright one, Nat," Salerno said, circling behind the robot.

"IF THAT IS THE CASE," Nat said, "I MUST LOCK DOWN ALL EXITS LEADING OUT OF THIS BUILDING."

He'd begun entering a code into a keypad on his left wrist, when he realized that Salerno was right behind him. "COMMANDER SALERNO, WHAT ARE YOU DOING? I CANNOT ALLOW YOU TO—"

Suddenly, his head drooped and his eyes went blank as Salerno pulled a wire from his back.

"I know you can't let me leave, Nat," she said. "But I can't allow you to stop me."

After starting up one of the lunar rovers, she opened the bay door and made her escape.

Chapter Five

Mission Control

Glen had been wandering around for a while, but being on his own wasn't as exciting as he thought it would be. A vendor offered to make him a balloon shaped like a spaceship, and a face painter asked Glen if he wanted to get into the launch spirit by adding some stars to his cheeks. These were things for little kids, though, so he just said, "No, thanks."

He was starting to wonder if he should head to the spectator stands, when he came across an open gate. On the other side was a building marked MISSION CONTROL.

Hmm, that could be interesting, Glen thought. He passed through the gate and—even though he wasn't sure if he was allowed in—entered the building.

Inside, he found a huge room filled with

computer monitors and television screens. It was here that the launch operations would be carried out. Oddly, though, for all of the equipment in the room, Glen saw only a couple technicians running it all.

"Sorry I can't show you around," said one of the technicians, hurrying past Glen. "We've got a lot of work to do to get this bird off the ground."

"Yeah," said the other technician as she operated two computers at once, "with no money left in the space program's budget, it's just me and Rollins left to do the work of fifty people."

"Well, there's also—" began Rollins, the first technician.

"Just what in tarnation is going on here?" a voice boomed. Glen looked up and saw a gruff-looking man with a gray crew cut storm into the room.

Swanson, the second technician, gulped and whispered to Glen, "That's Slayton. He's the flight director."

"Swanson! Rollins!" roared the approaching Slayton. Pointing at the largest television monitor in the room, he asked, "Why isn't anyone keeping an eye on Hatcher? He looks like he's about to lose his lunch!"

Glen looked up at the screen and saw that it was true. The video showed a live feed of a very queasy-looking astronaut in the rocket's flight capsule. The astronaut reminded Glen of how he looked that time he ate all his Halloween candy in one night.

"Sorry, sir," said Rollins.

"We're doing our best, sir," added Swanson.

"Well, your best isn't cutting it! You, there," said Slayton, turning to Glen, who felt his face turn red for the second time that day. "I don't know who you are or what you're doing here in Mission Control, but *someone* needs to keep that astro-flyer from tossing his cookies all over the flight capsule."

"Are you saying *I* need to do something about it?" asked Glen, wishing that he'd stayed with his dad. "I'm just a kid!"

"I don't care if it's a kid, an adult, or a rhinoceros! Someone needs to give that astronaut

something to calm his stomach before he makes a
mess up there and ruins this launch!"

"Y-you want me to go into the capsule?"
stammered Glen.

"Glad I made myself clear. Now get going!"

In a daze, Glen left Mission Control and walked
outside. His feet were carrying him in the direction
of the elevator to the flight capsule, but he had no

idea what he was supposed to do once he got
there. Suddenly, he remembered that he had a can
of ginger ale in his backpack. His dad had given it
to him before they left the house, saying it would
make Glen feel better if he got carsick. At the time,
Glen had told his dad that he hadn't been carsick
in years, but now he was glad that he'd taken it.
He just hoped that it would do the trick.

Glen reached the elevator to the flight capsule and stepped onto the platform. After pulling shut the grated metal door, he looked for the UP button. But he didn't see it—he didn't see any buttons at all. Instead, there was just a lever attached to the wall. Glen pulled it and immediately felt himself being whisked into the sky. It was much faster than any ordinary elevator—so fast, in fact, that Glen thought he might need the ginger ale to calm his own stomach. But just as suddenly as the elevator had begun to rise, it came to an abrupt stop. Glen took a second to allow his stomach to settle and then pulled the grated door open.

Glen carefully walked across the gangplank from the elevator to the capsule door. If he hadn't been a little afraid of heights, he might have looked down and tried to spot his dad hundreds of feet below. Instead, he concentrated on putting one foot in front of the other. At last, he reached the capsule perched atop the rocket and stepped inside.

"Ugh . . . I don't feel so good," moaned Hatcher, the ill astronaut. His face was green, and he held his helmet upside down below his mouth. He saw the surprised look on Glen's face and said, "For all the gadgets in this capsule you'd think they'd include a wastebasket."

"Uh, yeah, I guess you're right," said Glen. Not knowing what else to say, he took the ginger ale from his backpack and handed it to Hatcher. "Here, this might make you feel better."

Hatcher took the can and drank it down. As he did, Glen's eyes roamed around the tiny capsule. Although he was anxious to get back down to the ground, he couldn't help but think that it was pretty cool to be inside a real spaceship.

"Thanks a lot, kid," said Hatcher. His face had regained its normal color, but he still looked shaken. "I'm not sure what happened to me there. It must have been something I ate."

"Well, if you're feeling better, I guess I'd better be going," said Glen. "I'm sure you've got a lot to do before blasting off into outer space."

"Hold on a second," said Hatcher as Glen turned to go. The astronaut was beginning to sweat, and his eyes darted around the capsule.

"With all the budget cuts, I didn't get a whole lot of training to fly this thing, and . . . uh . . . I think I'd better go read over the operator's manual once more."

Hatcher handed his helmet to Glen and quickly left the capsule.

"Hey! Where are you going?" Glen shouted after the astronaut. "Aren't you supposed to be—?"

Suddenly, the door closed with a loud clang and the lights within the capsule began flashing red. The words LAUNCH SEQUENCE COMMENCING appeared on a screen near the instrument panel. Glen had little time to realize what was happening before he heard Flight Director Slayton's voice coming over the radio.

"Hatcher, if you're feeling better, it's time to get this show on the road."

"Mr. Slayton, it's me, Glen Johns! Hatcher left!" shouted a panicked Glen, hoping Slayton could hear him.

"Who?" asked Slayton, sounding very alarmed.

"The kid you sent to help Hatcher!" Glen

called, banging on the hatch and pulling with all his might. "Mr. Slayton, you've got to get me out of here!"

For several seconds, Glen heard nothing but beeping noises within the capsule and the rocket's engines coming to life. At last, Slayton responded.

"Okay, son, it seems we have a little situation here. Apparently, Hatcher's had a small case of the jitters and won't be able to complete this mission. Luckily, I believe you have the right stuff to carry it out."

"What?" shouted Glen. The lights within the capsule were flashing more quickly now. The engines roared, making it difficult for Glen to hear his own voice. "I'm just a kid. I don't know how to fly a spaceship!"

"You're not understanding me, son. This mission must be carried out, and I'm afraid we've already reached the point of no return. It's too late to abort."

Glen could hear an automated voice over the radio.

"Countdown commencing. Twenty, nineteen, eighteen . . ."

"Dad! Where's my dad?" yelled Glen. He just wanted this to be over, to wake up and realize it was all a bad dream.

"I'm here, Glen." Mr. Johns's voice came in through the speakers. He struggled to sound reassuring, knowing that it would do Glen no good to hear his father panic. "They told me what happened and brought me to Mission Control."

"Twelve, eleven, ten . . ."

"Dad, I'm so scared!"

"I know, Glen," Mr. Johns said, his voice quivering, "but if you just listen to Mr. Slayton and follow his instructions, everything will be okay."

"Dad!" shouted Glen. "I'm sorry I—"

"Son," interrupted Slayton, "you'd better put on that helmet and strap yourself in, *now*! This may be a bumpy ride."

"Three, two, one . . ."

Chapter Six

Liftoff

Glen had just strapped himself into his seat when he felt the tremendous thrust of the booster rockets. The force mashed his body back into the seat, making him feel like an elephant was sitting on his chest. For several seconds, Glen couldn't open his eyes, even if he'd wanted to. Instead, he could only hear the *whoosh* of the rockets as he flew skyward.

"Just hold on there, son," said Slayton, coming in through the radio. "You're passing through Earth's atmosphere, which is causing the capsule to shake."

Through gritted teeth, Glen managed to whisper, "How much longer?"

"You're almost through the first layer of the atmosphere and are about to enter the stratosphere," replied Slayton.

Glen kept his teeth clenched and hoped his head wouldn't explode. He tried to distract himself by slowly counting backward from ten, just like he always did when the dentist drilled a cavity. He only made it to seven, though, before Slayton's voice broke in again.

"You're just about through the stratosphere, son. Things should start to get easier from here on out."

It was true. The higher the ship flew, the less it shook, and the pressure on his body became less severe. Glen even managed to open his eyes for the first time and could see the blue sky outside growing darker. He was entering the upper levels of the atmosphere, just at the edge of outer space.

"Okay, son," said Slayton, "we're deploying the booster rockets in three . . . two . . . one!"

Glen felt a jolt as the rockets fell away from the capsule, dropping thousands of feet into the ocean below. The ship rolled, and Glen could see them falling toward the blue planet he'd just left.

"Dad, are you there?" asked Glen.

"Yes, Glen," responded Mr. Johns. "Is

everything okay? Are you hurt?"

"I'm fine, Dad," Glen answered. And as he watched his planet grow smaller and smaller in the

window, he added, "You wouldn't believe the view I have. Earth looks so different from up here."

Mr. Johns couldn't bring himself to respond.

He was happy to hear Glen's voice and know that his son was okay. But he wouldn't be able to feel any relief until Glen was back on the ground.

Glen was marveling at how tiny the Earth looked, when he caught something out of the corner of his eye. It was his backpack, floating in the capsule like a helium-filled balloon.

"Hey," said Glen, "my backpack is weightless!" Unstrapping from his seat, he reached out and poked his bag, which slowly careened off the capsule's walls.

"Affirmative," said Slayton. "Now that you're in outer space, you'll find that the capsule is free of gravity."

"Cool," said Glen, more to himself than anyone. He stared in fascination as the backpack slowly floated around the pod. Then, snapping back to the reality of where he was, he said to the flight director, "Well, Mr. Slayton, you got the ship off the ground, so now I guess it's time to bring me home."

"I'm afraid we can't do that just yet."

"What do you mean?" asked Glen, once

again feeling alarmed. "The space program's last mission was supposed to be one final launch. Well, you launched the ship, so I'm done and can come back home, right?"

"Negative. There's more to the mission than just the launch," answered Slayton. Mr. Johns, who was listening to the flight director, got a bad feeling in the pit of his stomach. He'd been afraid of this.

"What do you mean?" Glen asked.

"Yes, Mr. Slayton," Mr. Johns said, "what are you talking about?"

"One of our astronauts," Slayton began, "has been living on a lunar base for quite some time. We can't shut down the space program as long as there's someone still up there."

"Okay, fine," Glen said. "But what does that have to do with me? Why doesn't this astronaut just fly home?"

"This particular astronaut is Commander Rachel Salerno, who is . . . difficult," Slayton continued. "She has decided to carry out an unauthorized mission and has ignored all orders to shut down the facility and return home."

Mr. Johns braced himself for the worst and asked, "Mr. Slayton, what are you saying? Where are you sending my son?"

"Let me finish. Because of her resistance, it has become necessary to send someone to relieve her of her post and escort her back to Earth."

Glen hoped that "someone" wasn't him, but he dared to ask. "Mr. Slayton, are you telling me that I'm going—"

"To the moon, son. Your ship is taking you there now. Once on the ground, you must take Salerno into custody and return her to Cape Carpenter."

"Mr. Slayton," said Mr. Johns, sounding angrier than Glen had heard him in years, "you can't be serious! How can you send a thirteen-year-old boy to the moon?"

"This isn't fair," Glen added in protest. "You expect me to fly this ship to the moon and *then* capture an astronaut? I don't even care about your dumb space program! Why should this be my problem?"

Glen had never spoken this way to an adult

before, but he was mad. He couldn't believe what Slayton had told him.

"That ship of yours will take you straight into the moon's orbit, where a landing vehicle will take you to the ground. Mr. Johns, Glen, you can both relax," Slayton said. "Unless there's some unforeseen event, there will be no need to lift a finger. And, Glen, as far as your feelings about the space program go, you can be glad that the sooner you complete this mission and bring Salerno back to Earth, the sooner this 'dumb' program will be terminated."

Glen felt bitter about the situation he was in but was realizing that he had no option other than to do what he was told and get it over with. For his part, Mr. Johns sat with his face in his hands, wishing he and Glen had never come to Cape Carpenter.

"Now," Slayton went on, "I should warn you about Salerno. She is quite clever, and catching her may not be so—"

Wham!

Something hit the ship.

What the heck was that? Glen wondered.

Chapter Seven

An Unforeseen Event

"Asteroids!" shouted Slayton.

Glen's head was still a little foggy from the collision, but he knew that this wasn't a good situation. The red lights within the capsule were flashing again as a damage indicator blinked.

"You're in an asteroid field!" Slayton said. "You'll have to steer your way through it!"

"What?" Glen said, alarmed. "I thought I wouldn't have to do any flying!"

"This . . . no time . . . questions!" Slayton responded. The field was disrupting the radio signal, making it difficult for Glen to understand him. "Strap . . . seat and . . . get out . . . before . . . another collision!"

Glen knew he needed to do something, and fast. Through the window he could see hundreds of asteroids hurtling his way. Glen kicked off from the capsule wall and flew to his seat. He buckled himself in with no time to spare. He was headed right for a big one, which was large enough to smash his ship to pieces.

Flipping a switch on the command console, Glen changed the flight operation from AUTOPILOT to MANUAL. He grabbed the steering controls and banked right, narrowly avoiding the incoming asteroid.

"Whew, that was close!" he said. But Glen didn't have a chance to relax—a cluster of three smaller asteroids, each with the ability to do massive damage to his ship, was right in front of him. Glen veered to the left and then quickly to the right to escape the path of the first two, but the third one was coming in fast. Pulling back hard on the steering column, Glen put the ship in a steep climb. He braced for the impact, but after a second, he realized that he'd cleared the projectile, however narrowly.

"I think I did it!" Glen shouted. "I'm out of the asteroid field!" Glen was right. He could see in his rear window that it was now behind him. He was out of danger—or so he thought.

"That was some good flying, son," Slayton said, the transmission no longer disrupted. "But that first collision must have done some damage." Glen saw that Slayton was correct. The indicator was still beeping. "After you put that bird back on autopilot, I've got another job for you."

Now what? Glen thought, flipping the switch back from MANUAL to AUTOPILOT.

"Son, I'm afraid you're not going to like what I have to say, but our readouts are showing that one of your landing gears is stuck. Unless you get it unstuck, you'll never be able to land that thing safely back on Earth."

"Okay," Glen said, "is there some button I can push to fix it?"

"It's not that simple, son. You're going to have

to manually unjam that gear, and to do that, you need to be outside."

Glen groaned. "Are you saying I need to—?"

"Yes," Slayton said, cutting him off. "You're going to have to do a space walk to make that repair."

Once again, Glen couldn't believe his ears, but he knew that he had no choice in the matter. "Just tell me what to do, Mr. Slayton."

Slayton gave Glen his instructions. Before he knew it, the boy was once again unbuckled from his seat and floating in the capsule. He opened the hatch leading to the fuselage, which was the part of the ship separating the flight capsule from the rear engines.

Slayton said I should find what I need in here, Glen said to himself, floating through the fuselage storage area. He saw crates full of all kinds of equipment and, at last, found what he was looking for—a bin marked SPACEWALK MATERIALS.

Glen opened the bin and put on the special airtight suit Slayton had said he'd need. He also spotted a long hose, which he attached to a port on his belt. He floated on, holding the other end of the hose in his hand.

Now I just need something to pry that landing gear open, he said to himself. It didn't take long for him to find what he was looking for, a crowbar in a crate of tools. *This should do the trick.*

With everything he needed, Glen arrived at the moment of truth. He passed through the airlock and reached the exit hatch, where he saw a port for the other end of his hose. He attached it and gave it a few good tugs to see that it was secure.

Boy, I hope this holds. Otherwise, I might be floating in space forever. Glen swallowed hard and grabbed the handle of the hatch. "I guess this is it," he said, pulling down.

The door flew open, and Glen was sucked out into the dark nothingness of space.

"Aaaaah!" he yelled as he was catapulted away from his ship. But suddenly he stopped just as abruptly as if he'd run into a brick wall. Looking down at the rigid hose attached to his belt, Glen realized he was safe.

"It held!" he shouted. "The hose held!" Then, using one hand while the other clutched the crowbar, he began using the hose to pull himself back to the ship.

At first, Glen was afraid to let go of the hose again, but he soon found that, with a good, strong pull, he could send himself floating toward the fuselage. When he reached the outside of the ship, he put one hand on the bottom part of the hatch and swung himself down to the vehicle's belly, where he saw what he was looking for.

The underside of the ship was badly dented from the asteroid, and the panel covering one of

the rear landing gears had been shoved into the mechanism.

That doesn't look good, Glen thought, floating toward the damaged area. *But if I don't fix it, I'm in big trouble.*

With one hand, Glen reached up and grabbed the dented panel. Bracing himself against the ship, he pulled as hard as he could. It didn't budge.

"Darn!" he said. "It's really stuck. Okay, I guess I'd better try Plan B."

Glen stuck the crowbar into the landing gear and began trying to unjam the metal panel.

"Oof," he said. "I can't get enough leverage." Then, holding on to the crowbar with both hands, Glen put one foot on each side of the landing gear. Pulling with his entire body, he could feel every muscle quiver from the strain. Then, at last—

Creeeeaaaaak!

The bent metal gave way, making it possible to deploy the landing gears!

It may not be pretty, Glen thought, *but I think it's fixed!*

After returning to the fuselage and closing the

hatch behind him, Glen radioed Mission Control.

"Problem solved, Mr. Slayton."

Back home, everyone breathed a sigh of relief. Especially Glen's father.

Chapter Eight

Smooth Sailing

Glen made his way back to the capsule and strapped himself back into his seat. He'd always wondered what it would feel like to float in a zero-gravity environment, but now that he'd tried it, he just wanted a rest.

"Phew," he said as he fastened his seatbelt. He felt the bump on his head from when he'd crashed into the wall and saw that his hands were still shaking from all the excitement. Now, with no launch, no asteroid field, and no other crisis at hand, he sat back and tried to relax.

I can't believe I'm really in outer space, Glen thought as he stared out the capsule window. He'd never even visited another country, yet here he was outside Earth's atmosphere. As far as his eyes could see were the twinkling lights of distant stars and planets, all within a massive ocean of darkness.

Glen couldn't help but wonder how far outer space stretched, or even if it ended at all. And if there was an "end" to space, what then? Was there something else beyond it, or was there just nothing?

It made Glen's head hurt to try to wrap his mind around all of this, and at last he sighed, swiveling his chair away from the window.

Now, what's the deal with this Salerno character? Glen wondered, his thoughts shifting from the mysteries of the universe to the astronaut he was supposed to bring back to Earth. There had been times when he'd disobeyed his dad, like when he ate a bunch of junk food before dinner, but he couldn't imagine what would make an astronaut ignore her orders.

I guess it doesn't matter, he thought. *All I know is that I need to find her so I can get home. But still, what kind of unauthorized mission is she on?*

"This is Slayton," the flight director said, interrupting Glen's thoughts. "Do you copy?"

"Yes," Glen replied, shaking himself back to the present. "I copy."

"You're approaching the moon's orbit, so you'd better get back to the fuselage and enter the lunar lander," Slayton said.

Glen knew what Slayton was talking about. When he'd passed through the fuselage earlier, he'd noticed a small landing vehicle, which he supposed would take him to the moon's surface.

"Okay," Glen said. "Will I have to do anything?"

"That's a negative," Slayton answered. "All you have to do is sit there and enjoy the ride. Compared to what you've been through so far, it should be a piece of cake."

Chapter Nine

Salerno

The rover zoomed across the lunar surface, leaving clouds of dust in its wake. It had been wandering the northeast sector of the moon for hours, but its driver, Commander Salerno, felt no closer to finding Number Four than when she left the barracks.

Drat, she said to herself, *I know Number Four is around here somewhere, but it's like trying to find a tennis ball in a desert.* Salerno's face was grim with frustration. Then, spotting the outer slope of a nearby crater, her spirits rose a little. *Hmm, maybe seeing things from a different point of view would help.*

Salerno jammed her foot on the accelerator as the rover raced up the huge hill. She skillfully dodged the rocky debris that littered the slope and, at last, reached the rim of the crater.

Stepping out of the rover, she looked down

from the rim, far below into the crater's basin. Even after all these years on the moon, this lunar world never ceased to fascinate her. She stood for a moment in awe, wondering what it would have been like to see the moment of impact when a meteor had crashed into the moon, leaving behind this colossal hole below her.

"Okay, back to work," Salerno said, shaking herself from these thoughts. "Somewhere out there is Number Four. But where?" From high atop the crater's rim, she scanned the lunar surface in every direction. She could make out the faraway silhouettes of Numbers One, Two, and Three. She could also see the blinking lights of the distant mining facility to the west and the biodome to the north. Closest of all the lunar facilities was the medical building to the east. Otherwise, the moon's surface was barren, featureless but for the occasional crater that dotted the landscape here and there.

Salerno sighed, not knowing which direction to search next. "If only I had a Geiger counter," she said. "That device would lead me right to Number Four!"

Suddenly, Salerno caught sight of something out of the corner of her eye. Turning, she saw a pair of blue lights blinking high above the moon. They were very far away, but there was no doubt that they were descending, each second getting closer to the ground. Salerno peered through her binoculars to have a better look.

"Just as I thought," she said. "McNabb's errand runner has arrived." She watched the lunar lander make its way toward the landing pad outside the living quarters. As the vehicle touched down, Salerno wondered which astronaut was aboard.

"Is that you, Hatcher?" Salerno said aloud. "Have they finally taken off your training wheels and given you your own mission? Not likely. From what I've heard, you can't ride an escalator without getting queasy. No, I'm sure they've sent the best, someone with more experience. But who?"

Salerno paused. The door of the lander opened, and a figure, unidentifiable from such a distance, stepped onto the landing pad before entering the living quarters.

"Well, whoever you are, you have your job to do, and I have mine," Salerno continued. "You'll be coming for me, I suppose. I'm guessing you'll want to use a locator device to track me down." Salerno reached her gloved hand into her pocket and fingered the gadget she'd taken from the barracks. She looked in the direction of the medical facility before getting back into the rover.

As she pressed the ignition, she said, "Of course, finding me won't be so easy if the locator device is hidden."

Chapter Ten

Living Quarters

As Glen passed through the doors to the astronaut living quarters, he breathed a sigh of relief.

Maybe it's not Earth, he thought, *but at least I'm back on the ground.* Looking down the long hallway that lay before him, he said aloud, "Okay, Salerno, where are you?"

Glen began walking. He listened carefully for any signs of activity but only heard the echo of his own footsteps. Turning a corner at the end of the corridor, Glen found himself in a large room filled with empty tables, microwave ovens, and refrigerators.

"This must be where the astronauts eat," he said. "But where did everyone go?"

"They went home." It was Slayton, coming in through Glen's headset. "A couple years ago, this room would have been filled with astronauts grabbing some grub after a long day of research. With the budget cuts, though, they all got sent home. That is, all but Salerno."

Glen stood in the cafeteria, trying to imagine what it would have been like to see it filled with astronauts. He couldn't help but think about how lonely it would feel to be the only person living here.

"Mr. Slayton, I don't see Salerno."

"That doesn't surprise me," said the flight director. "She's a rail, barely took the time to eat anything. Always too busy with her work, she said."

"Then where do you think she might be?" Glen asked.

"Check the barracks," Slayton replied. "If you're lucky, you might catch her taking a nap, though I doubt it. She didn't sleep much, either."

Two more halls branched out from the cafeteria. The one to Glen's right had a sign that read VEHICLE BAY. The other, to Glen's left, pointed the way to the barracks.

Okay, Glen thought, *I guess this is the way.*

Glen walked slowly down the corridor, feeling

very on edge about being in the abandoned facility. If he heard so much as a pin drop, he might have jumped out of his skin. Halfway down the hall, Glen saw a door marked GYMNASIUM. He knew that Slayton had told him to check the barracks, but Glen's curiosity got the better of him.

"I wonder what's in here," he said as he opened the door. Entering, he found an enormous room filled with basketball hoops, trampolines, climbing ropes, and other equipment. It was a lot like the gym at his middle school back on Earth, but so much better.

"Look at this place!" he exclaimed. "No wonder Salerno doesn't want to come home." Glen picked up a basketball from the floor and shot a few baskets. Since he was still wearing his space suit, it didn't take long to work up a sweat.

Glen spotted something on the wall, which he assumed was a thermostat. *It's getting a little hot in here,* he thought. *I'd better turn the temperature down.* Flipping the switch to the left, Glen immediately felt his feet leave the floor.

"Whoa!" Glen shouted, surprised to find himself floating in the air. "What the heck is this thing?" He swam through the air until he hovered near the wall device. Looking at it more closely this time, he saw that it said GRAVITRON. "Cool! This thing must control the room's gravity."

Glen kicked away from the wall and flew toward the basketball hoop on the far side of the gymnasium. Jamming the ball into the basket, he shouted, "Slam dunk! Two points for Glen Johns!" He pushed off the rim, somersaulting through the air. "This is so cool!"

For several minutes he played, feeling freer and having more fun than he had in a very long time. In fact, he was experiencing the type of joy he hadn't felt since he was a—

"Kid!" shouted Slayton. "You've got a job to do. Now, enough fooling around like you're on the playground, and find that missing astronaut!"

"Yes, sir," said Glen. He floated back to the Gravitron and reset it to normal gravity.

As Glen's feet touched the ground, he felt a little silly for playing around like a child. He hadn't exactly acted like a thirteen-year-old who had an important job to do. Still, as he left the gymnasium, he couldn't help but wish he'd had just a little more time to play.

Glen shut the gym's door behind him and continued down the hall until he reached the barracks.

"Hello? Commander Salerno? Is anyone here?" Glen asked. Hearing no reply, he walked past row after row of empty bunk beds. With the departure of the astronauts, they had all been stripped of their linens. Glen spotted one, however, that still had a pillow and blankets.

So, this must be where Salerno sleeps, Glen thought. The bed was not made but, instead, was covered by a heap of blankets. "I guess if no one was around to tell me to make my bed, I wouldn't bother with it either," Glen said, turning away. Then he noticed something—the corner of an object sticking out from beneath the pillow. Pulling it out, Glen saw that it was a notebook. He flipped through the pages but couldn't figure out what most of the drawings and scribblings meant. Most puzzling was the question scrawled over and over throughout the book: *Where is Number Four?*

"I don't know what any of this means or what Number Four is, but I'll bet this notebook will come in handy," Glen said as he stuck it into the pocket of his spacesuit.

Near Salerno's bunk was something else of interest, a workstation covered in papers and empty cans of Astrofizz cola.

"Sheesh, what a mess," Glen said. "Not making your bed is one thing, but living like a pig is another." Among the hundreds of papers that littered the desk were more drawings, maps, and calculations. The same question—*Where is Number Four?*—was written on many of these papers and even scratched into the desk.

Hmm . . . , Glen thought, *Salerno seems obsessed with finding this Number Four. But what is it?* As he pondered this question, he ran his fingers up and down one of the many stacks of papers and accidentally caused it to topple over. The papers fluttered to the ground, revealing a computer monitor.

"Hello, what's this?" Glen said as he saw what was on the screen. It was an e-mail, the one Salerno had read before fleeing the living quarters. Glen read through it carefully, especially the mention of "little green men," hoping it would give him a clue to where she might have gone. When he was done, he closed his eyes and thought deeply, trying to put the pieces of the mystery together.

"Okay, so Salerno is so obsessed with finding this Number Four thing that she disobeys McNabb, the space program director, who's telling her to shut this place down and go home. He gets mad and says he's sending someone to come get her. I guess that would be me." Glen laughed. Before coming to the moon, the most responsibility he'd ever had was taking care of his neighbor's dog for a weekend, yet here he was now, astronaut-hunting. "So, she knew someone was coming, which explains why she ditched this place. But what's this about 'little green men'? That means aliens, right?"

Glen frowned. Did Salerno actually believe in aliens? And did she really think that finding Number Four would lead her to them? It all just seemed so crazy. Maybe, though, that's what happens when you live on the moon by yourself for a long enough time. Eventually you start to believe in things that aren't possible. But, then again, she had so many notes, so many maps and drawings. It was obvious she'd done a lot of research. *Could* it be possible that she was onto something?

Glen tried to shake this thought from his head, fearing that he was already starting to lose his own marbles. But he did have to wonder just what kind of person he was dealing with.

"Well, one thing's for certain," Glen said, getting up to leave the barracks. "Salerno's not here in the living quarters, which means she could be anywhere on the moon." Remembering a sign he'd seen earlier, he said, "Luckily, I think I know where I can find a car."

Chapter Eleven

Vehicle Bay

Glen opened the door to the vehicle bay, hoping he'd find something he could drive on the moon's surface.

"If I'm lucky, maybe there's a jet pack somewhere around here," he said as he scanned the vehicle bay. The garage wasn't very orderly. There were tools lying all over the place and heaps of spare parts strewn about. But then Glen saw what he was looking for, a lunar rover.

"It may not be a jet pack, but this should make it a lot easier to find Salerno," he said, thinking that it was a lot like the dune buggy he and his dad had once driven on the beach. Then, seeing an empty parking spot nearby, he added, "And it looks like I'll need it to even the odds. Salerno must have one, too!"

Glen tried pulling open the bay door, but

it wouldn't budge. *Maybe there's something in the rover that will do the trick,* he thought. Climbing behind the wheel, he looked over the dashboard and found a button marked DOOR. "Aha!" he said as he pressed it. But to Glen's disappointment and frustration, the door didn't move. Instead, a message appeared on the dashboard console's screen. It said **DOOR ACCESS DENIED. SYSTEM OVERRIDE REQUIRED.**

"Darn it!" Glen said as he got out of the rover. He paced the vehicle bay, wondering why everything had to be so difficult. "It's not enough that I flew a spaceship to the moon? Now I have to figure out how to override the system just to open some dumb door? What does that even mean?"

As he stormed around the garage, he noticed a piece of machinery that didn't look quite like the others. In fact, it looked more like—

"A robot," Glen said aloud. He walked closer, thinking that its drooped head made it look like it was sleeping. "I wonder if this thing works," Glen said. He couldn't find an ON button, and nothing happened when he banged on the robot's head. But something caught his attention: a wire hanging from the back of the machine. "Hey," he said, "it looks like someone unplugged it. I wonder what will happen if I plug it in here—"

As Glen inserted the end of the wire into an empty port, the machine came to life. Its large eyes became illuminated and its head rotated wildly in every direction.

"NO, COMMANDER SALERNO!" said the frantic robot. "THIS IS AGAINST PROTOCOL!"

"Hey there," said Glen, surprised by the robot's sudden movements. "Just settle down. I'm not Commander Salerno, but I need to know where she is."

The robot looked at Glen and seemed to come back to reality, like someone who'd just woken up from a bad dream.

"PLEASE FORGIVE ME,

SIR. I AM A LUNAR FACILITY HELPER ROBOT, BUT THE
ASTRONAUTS HAVE ALWAYS JUST CALLED ME NAT.
APPARENTLY, I BRING TO MIND AN INSECT CREATURE
YOU HAVE ON EARTH, THOUGH I AM AFRAID I DO NOT
UNDERSTAND THE CONNECTION."

"Nice to meet you, Nat," Glen said, feeling a
little funny. He'd never talked to a robot before.
"What can you tell me about Salerno?"

Nat's eyes dimmed a bit, making him look
sad. "MY DUTY IS TO ENSURE THAT ORDERS ARE
CARRIED OUT. WHEN COMMANDER SALERNO REALIZED
THAT I WOULD NOT PERMIT HER TO LEAVE THIS FACILITY,
SHE DISCONNECTED MY WIRING. IF SHE ESCAPED, THEN
I FAILED TO DO MY DUTY."

Glen felt sorry for Nat but needed to know
more. "What could you have done to keep her
from leaving?" he asked.

"MY PROGRAMMING ALLOWS ME TO SHUT DOWN
THE BASE, KEEPING ANYONE FROM OPENING THE
DOORS. BUT I FAILED TO DO IT, AND NOW I AM JUST A
FAILURE." Nat dropped his head, saying, "BOO-HOO-
HOO."

"Wait a minute, Nat. If you can lock the

doors, does that mean you can open them, too?"
Glen asked.

"YES, OF COURSE," Nat replied, perking up his
head.

"In that case, you still have a chance to help!
I need an override on the vehicle-bay door right
away," Glen said, running back to the rover. "I'm
going out to find Salerno!"

"YES, SIR," said Nat. His eyes had brightened
again, and he punched numbers into a keypad on
his wrist, causing the bay door to instantly open.

"Thanks," said Glen, who turned on the rover's
ignition. But before he could step on the pedal, the
robot zoomed over to him.

"COMMANDER SALERNO'S SUIT EMITS A TRACKING
SIGNAL. UNFORTUNATELY, YOU WILL NEED A LOCATOR
DEVICE TO TRACK THAT SIGNAL, AND I SAW HER TAKE IT
BEFORE SHE DEACTIVATED ME."

"Then how will I find her?" Glen asked. "The
moon is a pretty big place!"

"AFFIRMATIVE. BUT BECAUSE THE LOCATOR DEVICE IS
QUITE BULKY, SHE MAY HAVE CHOSEN TO HIDE IT RATHER
THAN CARRY IT WITH HER. IF YOU CAN FIND THE LOCATOR

DEVICE, IT SHOULD LEAD YOU TO HER. I WOULD HELP YOU, BUT I AM UNABLE TO LEAVE THIS FACILITY."

"Got it! Thanks, Nat."

Glen stepped on the accelerator and drove out of the vehicle bay. Before him stretched the lonely lunar surface, and somewhere out there, he hoped, was Commander Salerno.

Chapter Twelve

Mr. Johns

Slayton was on the phone when Mr. Johns stepped into the flight director's office.

"Yes, yes, Director McNabb," said Slayton, speaking into the mouthpiece, "everything is on schedule. We'll have Salerno back on the ground in no time."

As Slayton spoke, he motioned for Mr. Johns to sit in one of the chairs facing the desk, which Glen's father did with an air of exhaustion.

"Right," Slayton continued, "I assure you the kid will get the job done. I'll keep you posted. Good-bye."

As he hung up the phone, he looked at Mr. Johns, whose face was filled with concern. "What can I do for you?" he asked.

Mr. Johns was done wasting time. "I want you to bring my son home, Mr. Slayton."

"You know we're doing everything we can to make that happen," Slayton replied. "And just as soon as he finds Salerno—"

"Now, Mr. Slayton," said Mr. Johns. "I want my son home now. I'm sure finding this Salerno character is very important to you, but what's important to me is getting my son home safely. I want you to call off the mission and get him home. Now."

Slayton sat back in his chair and looked at Glen's father. Though he had no children of his own, the flight director could understand the fear that lined the man's face. Nonetheless, he was under orders and had a mission to complete.

"Mr. Johns," Slayton began, "I promise you that we're going to do all we can to get your boy home safely, but abandoning the mission and leaving Salerno up there just isn't an option. It's not an ideal situation, I know, but right now, your boy is our best hope for rescuing that astronaut."

"Rescuing her?" Mr. Johns asked, frustrated. "It seems to me that she doesn't want to be rescued. So, how can you put the safety of my son at risk?"

"Again, Mr. Johns," Slayton said, "we're going to get him home just as soon as we can. But with all the media attention, it wouldn't benefit anyone to bring him back before the mission is complete."

"Media attention?" Mr. Johns asked. "What are you talking about?"

"Haven't you seen the news?"

"I'm sorry, Mr. Slayton, I've been a little too busy worrying about my son to watch television."

"Well, let me show you," Slayton said. He picked up a remote control from his desk and turned on a panel of televisions that covered his wall. Each was tuned to a different live news channel, where the top story was *"Boy Astronaut Travels to the Moon."*

As Mr. Johns stared in astonishment at the screens, Slayton said, "Glen has gotten us the kind of media attention we haven't had in years. Suddenly, everyone is interested in the space program again. I mean, who knows? Maybe your kid is just what we needed to regenerate public interest."

"Mr. Slayton," Glen's father said, turning

back to the flight director, "are you using my son just to save the space program?"

"No, of course not," replied Slayton. "No one planned this, and getting Salerno back is of the utmost importance. Still, you have to agree that this could be a very good thing for all who wish to see the space program continue."

"Mr. Slayton, I am a space enthusiast. I've always believed that discovery is one of the most important parts of life. But nothing is more important than my son, not even the space program."

Tonight's Poll Question:

Is space exploration awesome?

| YES | 80% |
| NO | 20% |

Boy Astronaut a Hero?

"Mr. Johns, a lot of jobs are at stake here. A successful mission with lots of public interest could be just the thing to save them."

Slayton's phone began ringing, and he could see that it was McNabb. "I've got to take this call. Don't worry, Mr. Johns, we'll get your boy home."

As he answered the phone, Mr. Johns got up to leave, but he stopped as he reached the door and turned back to the flight director.

"Mr. Slayton?" Mr. Johns said.

"Yes, what is it?" Slayton said, covering the mouthpiece with his hand.

"I told you that the spirit of discovery is why I'm fascinated by space exploration. What about you, I wonder. Are you here to save my son and your missing astronaut, or are you just trying to save your job?"

With that, Mr. Johns walked out of the office, leaving Slayton to stare at the empty doorway and ponder the question.

Chapter Thirteen

Lunar Surface

The hidden locator device, the mystery of Number Four, Salerno. Glen didn't even know how to begin solving all of these problems, but as he raced the rover across the lunar surface, he was, at least for a while, not thinking about his troubles.

"Wheee!" he shouted. The rover zigged and zagged across the moon, leaving tire tracks behind in the dust. The rim of a small crater appeared straight ahead, and Glen pressed the pedal to the floor. The vehicle jumped forward, heading straight for the crater. As it zoomed up the slope, Glen held on tight to the steering wheel.

Vwooooom!

The rover was airborne, flying high above the crater. Glen let out a whoop as he looked down at the ground below. The moon's reduced gravity allowed the vehicle to glide perfectly to the crater's

far slope, where its four tires landed softly. Glen rolled down the slope, where he skidded to a stop.

"That was awesome!" he said, catching his breath. Then, as he wheeled the rover around to jump the crater again, he saw a shape in the distance, something rising from the ground. Curious, Glen set off to investigate.

As he neared the object, he saw what it was: a tall, pencil-like structure sticking out of the moon's surface.

"It's an obelisk," Glen said aloud. "We learned about these in school." He was right; it was an obelisk, a four-sided structure with a pointed top. "But what's it doing here on the moon?" Glen wondered.

He drove the rover right up to the structure and got out to have a closer look. What he saw surprised him. The stone obelisk was covered in strange carvings, pictures, and letters that Glen didn't recognize. He walked around to each side, trying to make sense of his discovery.

"This is weird," he said. "What does all this mean, and who put this thing here? It doesn't look like something man-made." Glen was filled with wonder. He'd never seen anything like it before. Or had he?

"Wait a minute," he said, pulling out Salerno's notebook. He flipped through the pages until he found what he was looking for: a drawing of this very object. "I knew I'd seen this before!" he said. "According to Salerno's notes, she calls this Number Two. And here are drawings of Numbers One and Three, which I'm guessing are somewhere else on the moon's surface."

Glen flipped to another page of the notebook, where he found a map of the moon. Salerno's penmanship was hard to read— Glen figured that you must not need good handwriting to become an astronaut—but he saw that there were three numbers spread out on the map.

"Hmm, each of these numbers must represent an obelisk. So, Salerno must think there's a fourth one somewhere out there— Number Four! But that still doesn't explain what they are or where they came from."

He looked back up at the strange structure in front of him and gazed at it for several minutes, fascinated. It was hard for him to leave it without first understanding what it could be, but he knew that he needed to get moving. Looking back at Salerno's map, he saw that she'd marked the location of each lunar facility. Not far from Number Two was the medical facility.

I'd better check there, he thought. *With any luck, I'll find the locator device. Or better yet, Salerno herself.*

Chapter Fourteen

Medical Facility

Glen passed through the medical facility, which was where the astronauts came when they were sick or injured. Ever since he had his tonsils removed when he was six, he'd hated hospitals. And now, as he passed by examination rooms full of medical equipment used to poke and prod, he realized that hospitals on the moon were just as bad.

Man, this place gives me the creeps, Glen thought. *I wanna get out of here.* He considered just giving up and searching somewhere else, but he knew he couldn't do that, not if he hoped to ever make it home. So, Glen took a deep breath and continued his search.

He was passing by a door marked RESEARCH AND EXPERIMENTATION, when he noticed a beeping noise coming from within the room. He slowly opened the door and peered inside. The beeping was definitely coming from somewhere nearby, but Glen's attention was drawn to something else. There, in front of a large mirror, was a contraption made of two discs situated on top of a base.

"Cool," Glen said, "it's a gyroscope trainer. Astronauts strap themselves inside of these things to learn how to tolerate space travel." Glen knew that his body had already been through a lot for one day, but he couldn't resist trying it out. He strapped himself in and pressed the ON button. Immediately, the gyroscope started spinning every which way.

The world around Glen was a blur, but as he spun, he saw something that shocked him. For only a split second, it looked like he could see through the large mirror, and there, in a room on the other side, was a woman!

Glen didn't know if the gyroscope was distorting his vision, but he frantically reached for the OFF button, until, at last, the spinning stopped.

He came to a halt and, after unstrapping himself, jumped down. Unfortunately for Glen, his

body wasn't done spinning, and his rubbery legs
gave way beneath him. Crawling across the floor,
he looked up and saw that the room was whirling
above him. But the mirror looked normal.

Still a little dizzy, he managed to pull himself
to his feet and put his face to the glass. Again,
nothing seemed strange. It was just a mirror, not a
window into a room. And he certainly didn't see a
woman.

"Hello?" he said, tapping on the mirror. "Is

someone there?" No one answered, but he did hear something else. The beeping noise was definitely coming from the other side of the glass.

Leaving the Research and Experimentation room, Glen turned left down the hall, where almost immediately he found another door, this one marked RESEARCH OBSERVATION.

Entering, he saw several chairs facing a large window that looked out upon the gyroscope in the room he'd just left. Glen was so astonished that he barely noticed that the beeping was now very loud.

"Oh my gosh," he said. "It's a two-way mirror! The researchers must use this room to observe the experiments without being seen." Then, overcome with an eerie feeling, he said, "There really was a woman here a minute ago. And that could only be one person!"

Glen popped his head out into the hall and looked up and down the corridor. He knew, though, that Salerno must be long gone by now. He sat down in one of the chairs in the observation room and shook his head in disbelief over how close he'd been to her.

"Shoot!" he said, once again feeling frustrated. "If only I'd come into this room first, I would have caught her. Right now I could be bringing her back home."

Glen was upset by his bad luck, but the longer he sat, the more irritated he got by the beeping sound.

"What is that noise?" he said, getting up. He couldn't tell exactly where it was coming from, but it was really getting on his nerves. "Be quiet!" he said, kicking the wall. Then, to Glen's surprise, his kick caused something to fall from the ceiling vent. It hit the ground with a thud.

Hey, what is that? Glen wondered, bending down for a closer look. It was a mechanical instrument, about the size of a brick. A wire stuck out of one end, and an arrow blinked red in time with the beeps that had bothered Glen so much. Picking it up and finding that it was surprisingly heavy, Glen realized what he'd found.

"It's the locator device," he said. Turning around, he noticed that the red arrow turned green. He took a few steps forward, out into the hall, and saw that the frequency of the blinks and beeps had increased. "It must be leading me to Salerno!"

With his spirits high once again, Glen exited the medical facility and hopped into his rover.

Chapter Fifteen

On Salerno's Trail

The rover raced across the moon, following the locator device's tracking signal. Glen looked down at the device, which he'd placed on the passenger seat, and saw that the green arrow was flashing more and more rapidly.

I guess I'm headed in the right direction, he thought. As he used his left hand to steer, he used his right to take out the journal and flip to the map. *It looks like the signal is leading me to something called the biodome. That must be where Salerno is hiding!*

Glen was happy, knowing that soon enough he'd have Salerno and be allowed to return home. With his foot pressed to the floor, he said, "I'm coming for you, Commander."

But then something distracted Glen, and he veered off his path to have a better look. It was another obelisk, identical to the one he'd seen before but with different engravings. Glen fumbled for the notebook and found what he was looking for.

"Aha!" he said. "Here it is, Number One. This must be the first structure Salerno found." He was mesmerized by the towering object and burned to know more about it. What did its strange engravings mean, how did it get here, and most importantly, what was it used for?

"Son, do you copy? I say, do you copy?" It was Slayton's voice. He'd been barking over Glen's headset for several minutes, but it was just now that Glen heard him, so fascinated was he by the mysterious structure in front of him.

"Yes, sir, I copy," Glen said, shaking himself from his daydream.

"Son, you're wasting time. Now, quit stalling and get back on track!" ordered Slayton.

"Yes, sir, I will. But what can you tell me about these stone structures I'm finding out here?" Glen asked.

"Jeez-a-loo!" Slayton shouted. "Don't tell me you're turning into Salerno and getting all mushy-brained over those things."

"No, sir, I'm not. I'm just wondering—"

"Well, stop your wondering," Slayton said. "I don't know what those things are, probably just natural rock formations. Truth is, I don't really care. What I do care about is finding that missing astronaut. Do you copy?"

"Yes, sir, I copy," Glen said quietly. He walked back to the rover, feeling torn. He *did* want to find Salerno and get home, but his curiosity was hard to ignore. Despite what Slayton said, there was no way those structures just *happened*. Someone or something put them there. But who? And why?

Glen tried to shake these questions from his

head as he drove. The green arrow of the locator device was now beeping wildly, and he saw the biodome up ahead.

Parking the rover outside, Glen stepped out and entered the building. Unlike the other facilities, which were filled with white corridors and many rooms, the biodome was just one open space. Plants crawled up the enormous glass walls all the way to the domed ceiling, which was also made of glass.

I think I've heard about this place, Glen said to himself. *This is where the astronauts grew their food and did experiments on vegetation.* He looked around and was astonished at the size of some of the vegetables. There were apples and tomatoes the size of basketballs. *That's amazing,* Glen thought. *I wonder why their fruits and vegetables grow so big. Maybe it has something to do with the moon's gravity.*

Glen was considering this when he noticed a spiral staircase, its rails covered in plant life. From the ground, Glen couldn't tell where the stairs led, but it looked like they practically reached the ceiling. He decided to make the long climb to investigate.

When he reached the top, high above the

ground, he saw a door marked STORAGE. Not knowing what he'd find on the other side, he took a deep breath and gently opened it.

Inside, he found an area used to keep all kinds of gardening equipment. And among the rakes, shovels, and bags of fertilizer was a woman with her back turned to Glen. She muttered to herself and appeared to be looking for something.

It was Salerno.

"It's got to be somewhere around here," she said, talking to herself, unaware that Glen was in the room.

Glen was astonished to finally be face-to-face, or at least face-to-back, with Salerno. But now that he'd found her, he realized he didn't know what to do.

"Ahem," he said, clearing his throat.

Salerno froze. Then, slowly, she stood upright and turned around to face Glen.

"Just as I thought," she said. "It was hard to tell as you were spinning around on the gyroscope, but now I see that I was correct. They sent a boy, no more than twelve years old, to disrupt my search."

"My name is Glen Johns, and I'm actually thirteen," he said nervously. "And, uh, you're supposed to come with me." Glen felt even stranger than he had when he'd spoken to Nat the robot. He wasn't used to giving orders to grown-ups, especially astronauts.

"I can't do that," Salerno said. "I'm on the brink of the greatest discovery ever made, and I must see this through."

"Does it have something to do with those obelisks out there?" Glen asked. He knew he was supposed to be taking her into custody, but he was dying for some answers.

Salerno looked at Glen, who was surprised to notice a certain kindness in her eyes. "Have you seen them?" she asked.

"I saw two of them. What are they? Where did they come from?" he asked.

"Glen, I believe they were left here millions of years ago, long before the dawn of man. I can't say for certain *who* left them here, but I can tell you that it was no one of our Earth."

"So, you're saying they were created by . . ."

Glen's voice trailed off. He couldn't bring himself to say it.

"Yes, Glen, I believe they were created by aliens. And I think that if I can find the fourth obelisk, which I call Number Four, they may interact with each other in a way that will allow us to make contact with their creators."

Glen was fascinated by what Salerno was saying but was also aware of how crazy it sounded. And as much as he wanted to hear more about the obelisks, he knew that he had a job to do.

"Commander Salerno, I'm sorry, but I can't go home without you. Please, just give up your search and come with me."

The astronaut turned an empty bucket upside down and sighed as she had a seat.

"Glen," she began, "I've wanted to be an astronaut all my life, ever since I was a little girl. And do you know why?"

Glen didn't reply.

"It's because I wanted to explore the universe, to see what's out there. When I was a kid, I'd lie in the grass and stare up at the stars, trying to comprehend the vastness of space. And I asked the same question that's been asked throughout our history: *Are we alone?* Now I'm so close to proving that we are not alone, that there are others out there. I can't give up now."

Glen remained quiet, but he couldn't help thinking of his father. Mr. Johns would have understood what Salerno was saying. He'd be glad to know that there were astronauts like Salerno, who shared his sense of wonder and desire to know what other worlds might exist out there. In fact, Salerno's words reminded Glen of the way he once felt, when he was a young boy who was fascinated by space and all its mysteries.

"The space program is coming to a close, Glen," Salerno continued. "If I give up and leave with you now, I'll never get another chance at this. Do you understand?"

She searched the boy's face and saw that he was torn between what he wanted to do and what he had to do. Salerno felt sorry for him but had an idea.

"You know, Glen," she said, "I could use some

help in finding Number Four. Why don't you join me?"

"You want me to help you? But if you haven't found the fourth obelisk yet, what makes you think I could?"

"Well, you managed to track me down, didn't you? You must be pretty smart," Salerno said, causing Glen to blush. "Plus, I've been looking for a Geiger counter. It's a device that picks up signs of nearby radiation. If you could help me find it, I'm sure we'd find Number Four in no time!"

Something had awoken in Glen. He desperately wanted to join her, find Number Four, and see if Salerno was right about it being linked to alien life. But most of all, he wanted to explore. He was just about to answer her when Slayton's voice came in over his headset.

"Son, you've got her. Now bring her back to the lunar lander and come on home!"

Salerno heard Slayton's orders, too. She looked Glen in the eyes, waiting to see what his decision would be. At last, Glen hung his head and sighed.

"I'm sorry, Commander, but I really have to

get back to Earth. You need to come with me."

"I see," Salerno responded. "You have a job to do and don't want to disappoint the people back home." Salerno rose from her seat and began moving toward the wall. "But, Glen, I have a job to do as well, and I must do it. Not just for myself, but for everyone in the world who's ever wondered if there's life beyond Earth."

"Commander," Glen said, his voice cracking, "I really just want to go home. Please don't make this difficult."

Salerno reached for a switch on the wall and turned to Glen. "It is difficult, Glen. It's difficult because I see in you a young man who is turning his back on his spirit of exploration. I find that very sad." At that, Salerno pulled the wall switch, causing an airlock to fly open. Standing on the edge, she added, "I really wish you were on my team, Glen."

And then she jumped.

Glen ran to the edge and looked down, where he saw Salerno land softly on the moon's surface. She hopped into her rover and drove off.

"What's going on there?" Slayton demanded. "Do you have Salerno?"

"No, Mr. Slayton, she's escaped."

"Well, what are you waiting for?" he shouted. "Get after her while she's still close!"

Chapter Sixteen

Pursuit

"Just what in the world happened back there?" Slayton asked, sounding very angry. "I didn't figure you to be one to go screwy when the chips were down."

Back in the rover, Glen drove as fast as he could. His eyes were glued to the far-ahead lights of Salerno's fleeing vehicle.

"You don't have to worry about me, Mr. Slayton. I'll get her, and she won't get away this time."

The truth was, Glen didn't know what had happened. He'd been so close to catching her, to completing his mission and going home. But all that talk of obelisks, aliens, and discovery had distracted him.

She tricked me, Glen thought, feeling foolish for having allowed himself to get swept up in Salerno's fantasies. *But it won't happen again.*

Glen flew across the moon's surface, making up ground on Salerno. As he closed in on the lights up ahead, he began imagining what he'd say to her, promising himself that this time he wouldn't give her a chance to escape. But then, suddenly, the lights of Salerno's rover disappeared.

"Darn it!" Glen shouted. "She turned them off." Left behind in Salerno's trail of dust, Glen had no idea which way she'd gone. He slowed his vehicle to a stop, looking in every direction. Then, an idea occurred to him.

"You can run, but you can't hide," he said, turning on the locator device. The green arrow immediately began beeping, and Glen set off at once, following the signal until he reached a building he hadn't seen before.

I don't see Salerno's rover anywhere around here, Glen said to himself, patrolling the outside of the building, *but she must be here. The locator device is beeping like crazy.*

Glen stepped out of his vehicle and entered the building. He was surprised by what he saw. There seemed to be an infinite tangle of conveyor belts crisscrossing throughout the room. Glen had to duck his head under some of them. They carried massive rocks, all steadily rolling along until being fed into enormous machines, which ground them down before spitting out their dust.

"It looks like this is some sort of mining facility," Glen said, barely able to hear his own voice above the hum of the machinery. "I guess those machines grind down the rocks and extract their minerals. But where do all the rocks come from?"

Glen soon had his answer. The wildly beeping locator device led him down, down, down through a long tunnel into a cavern far below the moon's surface. Machines swinging pickaxes chopped away at the cavern walls, causing large pieces of rock to fall onto the ground. Different machines, these with shovels, then scooped up the fallen pieces and put them onto the conveyor belt leading back up the tunnel.

At any other time, Glen might have been interested in watching the mining operation. But

now he had only one thing on his mind: Find
Salerno! Glen looked down at the locator device
and saw that the arrow was flashing white.
Looking up, he saw a garage-style door. *I have you
now!* Glen thought, pulling it up.

But Salerno wasn't there. Instead, it was just a
room full of mining machines, many covered with
dust cloths. And spinning around in the middle
of the room was a malfunctioning robot with a
beeping gadget tied to its back.

"It's the signal," Glen said, furious. "Salerno
took the tracking signal from her suit and attached
it to this robot!"

He saw that there was something else tied to
the robot: a note.

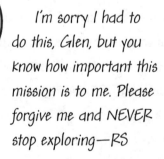

I'm sorry I had to
do this, Glen, but you
know how important this
mission is to me. Please
forgive me and NEVER
stop exploring—RS

"Darn it!" he shouted. "She tricked me again!" Angrily, Glen kicked a rock. "Ouch!" he wailed, hopping around on his other foot. "I hate this place!"

He sunk to the ground, hanging his head low. Glen had had enough of this moon adventure and just wanted to go home. Two hundred thousand miles away from Earth and all alone, Glen thought about everything that had gone wrong.

"That Salerno is such a cheater," Glen said aloud. "She fooled me into following her here. Now she could be anywhere. And why am I even here on the moon? If Slayton had just stopped the launch, or if Hatcher hadn't been such a chicken, I

wouldn't be in this mess."

Glen was feeling so sorry for himself that he felt his eyes moisten. As a single teardrop rolled down his cheek, he said, "But this is really all Dad's fault. If he hadn't dragged me to Cape Carpenter in the first place, none of this would have happened. He knew I didn't want to go!"

Glen sat for a long time feeling this way, thinking of everyone who was responsible for his troubles. Eventually, though, he ran out of people to blame.

"Well," he said, "I guess I could have just stayed with Dad. If I hadn't insisted on going off on my own, I never would have ended up in Mission Control. And if I hadn't gone to Mission Control, I wouldn't have been sent to help Hatcher." Glen considered this, how all his troubles began as soon as he left his dad's side.

Sheesh, he thought. *Why didn't I just stay with him? After all, he was only trying to spend some time with me. I bet he's worried sick now.*

Glen sat for another minute, imagining how hard this must be for his dad. At last, he stood up and said, "No, this isn't Dad's fault, and blaming everyone else isn't going to get me home any sooner. I have to find Salerno!"

But how?

Glen didn't know how he was going to find her when, by this point, she could be anywhere on the moon. But he did know that he needed to get going. First, though, he wanted to wipe the tears from his eyes.

Glen grabbed one of the dust cloths covering a nearby piece of machinery and used it to dry his face. As he pulled the sheet back, he was astounded by what he saw.

"Oh my gosh! It's the Geiger counter!" Glen exclaimed.

It was true. Under the cloth was the very instrument Salerno had been looking for.

"Well done, son," said Slayton, who had heard Glen over his headset. "That's a critical find. If you can use it to find that Number Four thing, you should be able to draw Salerno out of hiding."

Glen heard Slayton but was already running back through the mining facility to reach his rover outside. He didn't need to be told that the Geiger counter could help him lure Salerno from wherever she was. All he needed to do now was find Number Four.

Slayton said, "I see you're already on the move. And I also see from your suit's body readout that your adrenaline is sky-high. You sure must be excited to catch Salerno."

"Yes," Glen responded, "I am excited to find Salerno." But that wasn't the only thing he was excited to find.

Chapter Seventeen

Number Four

When Glen first left the mining facility, the Geiger counter made a clicking sound every ten seconds. But now, with that building far behind, the time between clicks was down to five seconds.

I must be getting close, Glen thought as he drove. With one hand on the wheel, he grabbed Salerno's notebook and checked the map. *It looks like I'm headed for the northeast area of the moon.*

He continued driving, listening for the clicks to guide his path. They were now coming every four seconds . . . three . . . two . . . one . . . until at last, Glen couldn't tell when one ended and another began.

The trouble was, he didn't see anything. There was no obelisk, no building, no Salerno. Instead, there was just the barren, rocky grayness of the moon.

Hearing the space between clicks return to one second, Glen circled back but still saw nothing.

"It should be right here," he said as he allowed the rover to slowly drift forward. "Why don't I—?"

Just then, Glen felt one of his front tires hit something. He backed up and got out to see what it was.

It didn't look like much, just a small triangular rock. But there was something odd about it. Glen grabbed a shovel from the back of his rover and began digging around the rock. After digging several inches down, Glen realized what it was.

"It's Number Four!" he shouted. "The rest of it must be underground. But how am I going to dig all the way to its base?" Glen wondered. "It will take me a year with this little shovel."

Then Glen got an idea. He'd noticed a winch on the front of his rover and attached its hook to the top of the buried obelisk.

Getting behind the wheel of his vehicle, he

said, "Okay, I hope this works."

Glen put the rover in reverse and stepped on the accelerator. The wheels spun, kicking up clouds of dust. "Darn! It's not working," Glen said. But he didn't give up. Instead, he pressed the pedal all the way to the floor. The vehicle groaned from the strain, and the metal cord of the winch looked like it could snap any second. "Come on, rover. You can do it," Glen said.

Just then, the vehicle began to inch backward, and to Glen's delight, he saw that it was pulling the obelisk from the ground.

"Yes! It's working," Glen shouted. "I—"

Snap!

The cord broke in two, causing the rover to fly backward.

"Shoot!" Glen said, slamming on the brakes. But then, as the huge cloud of dust began to settle, Glen saw what was happening. Number Four was rising from the ground on its own!

"I don't believe it," Glen said aloud to himself as he watched Number Four climb higher and higher, unassisted. He jumped out of the rover and ran to the obelisk, which now stopped at its full height.

"I did it!" Glen said, looking up at the towering structure. "I actually found Number Four! But now that I've found it, what do I do?"

Then, as though in answer to Glen's question, the triangular peak of Number Four began to glow. Suddenly, it shot a brilliant beam of light straight out across the moon's surface. Amazed, Glen looked out into the distance, where he saw the other three obelisks, each doing the same.

For a moment, Glen tried to process what he was seeing: four beams of light, each projected from an obelisk. Far away to the left was Number One. Straight ahead, many miles in the distance, was Number Two. Number Three was to Glen's right. And finally, where he stood was Number Four.

Then, his eyes brightening, Glen looked from one to the other and realized what he was seeing.

"An intersection!" he exclaimed. "I think I know where I need to go next."

Glen took off in his rover, following the beams of light until he reached the spot where they met. He was not surprised to see that he was not the only one there. Salerno was standing next to her own rover, shaking her head as she watched him approach.

"You did it," Salerno said, looking at Glen in amazement. "You found Number Four. And look," she said. "These beams of light, they form an *X*, like on a treasure map."

Glen walked over to Salerno, and they both stared at the point on the ground where the beams met. They were silent, but both wondered the same thing: *What was down there?*

"Son, do you have her?" Slayton said, his voice coming through over Glen's headset. "Do you have Salerno in custody?"

Both Glen and Salerno heard Slayton's question, and for a moment, they just looked at each other as the flight director continued to ask what was going on. At last, Salerno spoke.

"Well, so now what?" Realizing that she was lucky to escape from Glen three times already,

Salerno was prepared for the worst. After coming so close to unlocking the mysteries of the obelisks, she knew that she might never find out if her theories about alien life were correct. She held her breath as she waited for Glen's decision.

He grabbed two shovels from the rover, tossing one to Salerno. "We start digging," he said.

Salerno's eyes brightened as Slayton barked over the radio: "Mission Control requesting information! I repeat, do you have Salerno in custody?"

"Mr. Slayton," Glen said, looking at Commander Salerno's smiling face, "I'm afraid I've had to put your mission on hold for the moment."

"On hold?" Slayton roared. "Son, what do you think you're doing?"

"Well," Glen replied, "I guess I'm disobeying orders." He figured that would send Slayton over the edge, but the voice that responded over the radio wasn't the flight director's.

"Glen, can you hear me?" It was Mr. Johns.

Glen and Salerno were about to start digging, but hearing his father's voice made Glen pause. "Yes, Dad, I can hear you."

"Glen, I know you've been through a lot up there, but why don't you and Commander Salerno just follow orders and come home?"

Glen could hear the worry in his father's voice and was sure that his dad had been through a lot, too. He looked down at his feet and kicked a pebble, hoping that what he was about to say wouldn't upset his dad further.

"I'm sorry, Dad, but there's something we have to do first."

"But why?" Mr. Johns responded. "What could be more important than coming home?"

"Dad, it turns out that you were right. There's a lot left to explore in this universe, and it would be a shame to stop now, especially if this is the last chance we'll get."

Mr. Johns had been desperate to get Glen home safely ever since the launch, but hearing his son's words made him smile. It seemed that his spirit of discovery lived on.

"Okay, Glen, but be careful," Mr. Johns said.

"I will, Dad."

"Son?" Slayton's voice returned.

"Yes, Mr. Slayton?" Glen answered.

"Make us proud."

Chapter Eighteen

Alien Base

Glen and Salerno began digging at the point where the beams of light met. They had no idea what they might find, which made their work all the more exciting.

"Wow," Salerno said, sticking her shovel into the ground. "The soil here is so fragile. It's almost as if—"

"Move!" Glen shouted. They both jumped back as the ground beneath them gave way, creating a massive hole.

Glen and Salerno peered into the darkness and were astounded by what they saw. A coiled staircase led deep beneath the moon's surface. They heard the fallen rocks land far, far below, but through the darkness, they could see a faint light.

"What do you suppose is down there?" Glen asked.

"I'm not sure," replied Salerno, grinning. "I guess there's only one way to find out."

Glen smiled back and asked, "Are you ready?"

"You bet," said Salerno, who was already descending the stairs. "Try to keep up."

Glen followed close behind her, wishing that there were rails along the stairwell. Even with the moon's reduced gravity, he didn't want to imagine what it would be like to fall, especially since he had no idea what he might find at the bottom.

The pair descended hundreds of feet, both running their hands along the surprisingly smooth outer wall of the hole. It felt almost like marble. As they neared the bottom, the light that had once been faint grew brighter until they reached the floor.

There, they saw the source of the light. Along the walls of an enormous arched tunnel were glowing orbs, balls of light that hovered in the air.

"Cool! What are these things?" Glen asked, gently poking one, causing it to slowly glide away.

"I don't know, but look at this!" Salerno said, pointing at something on the tunnel wall. "It's a picture."

Glen came alongside the commander and saw what she was looking at. It showed a stick figure standing next to a large circle. Like the mysterious engravings on the obelisks, it was etched into the surface of the wall.

"What do you suppose it means?" Glen asked. The two looked at it for a long time, trying to figure out what it could represent.

"I have no idea," Salerno said at last. "But look," she said, pointing at the tunnel wall. "Another one!"

As Glen and Salerno approached it, the glowing orbs followed, providing light for the second picture.

"It's just like the first one," Glen said, "but in this one the stick figure is standing inside the circle." He stood looking at it, wondering what it meant, when Salerno, who had already gone farther down the tunnel, called him.

"A third one," she said. "And I think it's starting to make sense." Glen and the orbs followed Salerno, whose eyes were now sparkling. "See? This one shows the stick figure standing on the other side of the circle. And look what else!"

Glen saw what she was talking about. The picture showed a group of taller stick figures. It almost looked as though they were greeting the first one, but Glen couldn't be sure. Also confusing was the other image in the picture. To the right of the taller stick figures was an obelisk like the ones he'd seen on the moon's surface.

"I still don't get it," Glen said. "What does this all mean? What is this place?"

"Don't you see, Glen?" Salerno replied. "They've been waiting for us."

"*They?*" Glen asked. "You mean the aliens?"

"Yes!" Salerno responded. "Thousands, or maybe even millions, of years ago, they visited the moon and built this base. They've been waiting ever since for us to develop the technology to find it."

Glen didn't know how Salerno was getting all that from pictures of some stick figures and circles, but she seemed so sure of what she was saying.

"Okay," he said, "but what do you think they want?"

Salerno looked at the engraving, her eyes filled with joy, and said, "I think they want us to visit them."

"Visit them where?" Glen asked, trying hard to follow Salerno's logic. "Are they still here?"

"No," Salerno said, "I'm sure they left long ago, but I think they want us to journey to their planet."

Glen gulped. He'd been eager to search for alien life, but he hadn't been prepared for traveling to another planet!

"And how do you know all this?" he dared to ask.

Salerno was already walking back to the first engraving. Pointing at it, she said, "Look at this picture, Glen. This figure represents us, human beings. It's standing on the outside of this circle." She continued to the second engraving, Glen following close behind. "Then, we see the figure *inside* of the circle. Somewhere around here must be some vehicle or other means of transport, because look," she said, now showing Glen the third image, "the figure has exited the circle, where

he's greeted by these others. They must be the aliens."

"And what about the obelisk in the picture?" Glen asked. "What do you think that means?"

"Well," she said, "we saw the ones they left here on the moon. I'll bet their world is filled with them."

"So, what do we do now?" Glen asked, not sure he really wanted to know the answer.

"We have to find out how to reach their planet. And I think I know where to look next. See?" Salerno said, pointing.

Glen saw what Salerno was seeing. The glowing orbs had floated on to a spot on the wall, where they formed the outline of a door.

"They're leading us," Salerno said. "Come on!"

Glen and Salerno walked to the orbs, one overjoyed with excitement, the other filled with doubt. Reaching the spot outlined by the balls of light, Salerno reached out her hand and was astounded to find that her hand went right through the wall, as though it wasn't there at all.

Turning to Glen, she said, "Are you coming with me?"

Scared, but curious to find out what was on the other side, Glen said, "I'm right behind you."

Passing through the portal, Glen and Salerno found themselves in an enormous domed chamber. Suspended along the walls were hundreds of glowing orbs, just like the ones they'd seen in the tunnel. And hovering above the floor in the middle of the room was another orb, this one different from the others. It was smaller, only about the size of a marble, but it glowed with an intensity that made Glen and Salerno squint. As they approached it, they both experienced a strange sensation. It seemed to be drawing them nearer, like a magnet.

"This doesn't seem safe," Glen said, backing away. He could see strands of Salerno's hair floating toward the tiny orb. "Commander Salerno, I don't feel good about this."

"Glen," she replied, "I don't think there's anything to fear. And besides, aren't you curious to know what this is?"

Glen was curious, but he couldn't bring himself to go any nearer. Noticing something odd on the far side of the room, Glen found a good reason to get away from the small ball of light.

"Hey," he said, "I found something. I'm going to check it out."

While Salerno stayed with the orb, transfixed, Glen crossed the room. There, against the wall, he found a button.

"Do you have any idea what this might be?" he asked, calling to Salerno.

"I think I do, Glen. You'd better push it."

"But how can you be sure it's safe?" he asked, nervous about what it might do.

"We can't really be sure about anything, Glen, unless we're sometimes willing to take a leap of faith. Please, just trust me."

Reluctantly, Glen pushed the button.

Immediately, the orbs along the walls cast beams of light in the direction of the glowing ball in the middle of the room. The tiny orb expanded, growing so quickly that in a second it was a hundred times its original size.

"What's going on?" Glen shouted, shielding his eyes from the bright lights. The orb was becoming enormous, filling the middle of the room and swallowing up Salerno like a speck of dust in a huge bubble.

"It's okay, Glen," she shouted from within the blinding sphere.

"No!" Glen called to her. "You've got to get out of there!" He was panicking, unsure of what he'd just done. He shielded his eyes from the intensity of the light, but he could hear Salerno reply.

"I can't do that, Glen," she called. "I've got to find out what's on the other side! And besides, they've been expecting me for a long time now."

And as she said this, the orb collapsed in on itself and was gone, taking Salerno with it. Unable to believe his own eyes, Glen stood alone in the now-quiet empty chamber.

"Mission Control requesting status update," Slayton said. "I repeat, Mission Control requesting status update! Are you there, son?"

"Yes," Glen said, in a daze, "I'm here, Mr. Slayton."

"And Salerno? What's her status?" the flight director asked.

"I've lost her," Glen said. "She's gone."

Slayton was quiet for a moment, but at last, he sighed and said, "Son, you did a good job up there. I'm sorry to hear about Salerno, but I think it's time for you to come home."

Chapter Nineteen

Back Home

Glen's trip back to Earth was very somber.
For so long he'd wanted nothing other than to go
home, but now, he could only think about Salerno,
wishing he could have done something to save her.
As he began his reentry into the atmosphere, he
imagined how much happier he'd be if his friend
were returning to Earth with him.

After touching down on the landing pad, Glen
opened the hatch of his capsule and stepped out
onto the gangplank leading to the elevator. As he
rode down, he was surprised by what he saw below.
Thousands of people had assembled, and they were
all cheering for him.

Where did all these people come from? Glen
wondered as he reached the ground. Passing
through the crowd, Glen felt many pats on the
back and saw signs saying things like WAY TO GO,

GLEN and WELCOME BACK, HERO.

Inside Mission Control, Rollins and Swanson stood and applauded as Slayton greeted Glen.

Shaking hands, the flight director said, "Welcome home, son. We're awfully proud of you."

"Great job," said Rollins.

"Good to have you back," added Swanson.

It was nice to be welcomed back by the people in Mission Control, but Glen really just wanted to see his dad, who was standing behind the others.

He walked up to Glen and, knowing that his teenage son might otherwise be embarrassed, extended his hand. But Glen, who was finally realizing all that he'd been through, threw his arms around his dad, and for a long moment Slayton, Rollins, and Swanson looked on as father and son shared a tearful embrace. They were so moved by the scene that no one noticed the printer attached to the radio receiver spitting out a sheet of paper.

"I'm so sorry, Dad," Glen said. "I never should have left you."

"It's okay, Glen. I'm just happy to have you back."

"Dad, you were right," Glen said, still clutching his father. "The universe is so big. There's so much out there to explore."

Mr. Johns smiled, his eyes still wet. "I'm glad you got to see some of it before it was too late."

Glen let go of his father and spoke to everyone in the room. "I just wish I could have brought Commander Salerno back with me. You wouldn't believe what we discovered."

"She was a brilliant astronaut," Slayton said, "and will be missed." Everyone nodded in agreement, sorry that she was gone.

But then Rollins noticed something—the paper that had just come out of the printer. "Hey, everyone, what do you think this means?" he said.

"It's Morse code," Swanson said, looking at the paper. "I think I can make it out."

They all gathered around as Swanson decoded the message.

Sorry for all the trouble, guys, but I made it. Glen, it's more beautiful here than I'd ever imagined. Maybe you can visit me here someday—RS

Everyone in the room stared at each other in astonishment. A grin crept across Glen's face, and he thought, *She made it. She actually made it!*

"But what does this mean?" Rollins asked. "Did Salerno—?"

"I'll tell you what this means," a voice said. They all looked up and saw Roger McNabb enter the room. Slayton braced himself, realizing that he could be in real trouble for failing to bring Salerno home. But before he could offer an explanation, McNabb said, "This means that the space program is saved. Salerno's discovery and this young man's bravery have rejuvenated people's interest in space. Have you seen the crowd out there? Well, the president has, and he's decided to restore all the funding we need to keep the program going."

They all let out a cheer as McNabb added,

"Young man, why don't you go out there and let the people see what a real hero looks like?"

"This is pretty cool, isn't it, Glen?" Mr. Johns asked his son as they walked toward the exit.

"It is, Dad," Glen said. "But next weekend maybe we can just go fishing instead."

Turn the page for a sneak preview of

Poptropica®

cryptids ISLAND

available now!

« NEWS FLASH! »

Hey-ya, listeners, welcome to WADV AM Radio and The Adventure Hour with your courageous, audacious, and fearless host—me!—Illinois Johnson.

Buccaneers, have I got a scoop for you. This isn't just breaking news—this is smashing, shattering, splintering news!

Are you ready for it? Here goes . . .

Eccentric billionaire Harold Mews is about to announce a contest for "treasure hunters and seekers of fame, fortune, and glory from across the globe."

The details of the contest are as yet undisclosed, but one week from today, all will be revealed! Harold Mews will make the announcement from the Mews mansion in Bucky Cove.

So all you globe-trotting thrill seekers—be there or be left out!

For now, this is Illinois Johnson signing off from WADV AM—the radio home for adventurers, swashbucklers, and thrill seekers!

Chapter One

Flyby

Annie Perkins adjusted the propane burner and heard the familiar *whoosh* of flame as the hot-air balloon climbed higher into the sky. She tilted the outboard motor's propeller (that was of her own special design, allowing her perfect control of the balloon), and the balloon picked up speed, moving swiftly through the air, surrounded by nothing but bright blue sky.

Annie checked the height gauge. She was 379 feet up in the sky, but she was as calm and relaxed as if she were lying poolside. Annie was comfortable by herself—she always had been. And that's why she knew she'd go down in history as a legendary adventurer.

"Getting close, now," Annie said aloud.

The small bay town of Bucky Cove was coming into focus. Treetops and the slanted crests of houses and shops dotted the horizon. As the balloon floated closer, Annie could even make out the famous MEWS FOUNDATION sign atop Harold Mews's mansion.

Harold Mews—Annie's hero . . .

It was one week earlier that Annie had made the decision to travel to Bucky Cove and enter the contest. She had been washing dishes at Perkins Dine-In, the small restaurant her family owned. As usual, Annie was listening to WADV AM Radio—it was *The Adventure Hour with Illinois Johnson*. That day, Illinois had broadcast news that grabbed the attention of adventurers across the globe—news about Mr. Harold Mews's million-dollar contest!

Annie could hardly believe her ears. *One million dollars!* Perkins Dine-In was in trouble, and Annie knew that if her family failed to pay back the loans, it wouldn't be long before the bank took away the restaurant. One million dollars would be enough to save it!

Annie told her parents she planned to enter

the contest—but they were *not* having it. "You don't even know what the contest will be!" her mother had exclaimed. "No one does! That Harold Mews is a reclusive nut!"

Annie had just smiled at that, because Annie knew more about Harold Mews then anyone! Since she had been old enough to lift a book, Annie had been reading about Mews's exploits: his journeys deep into the Sahara, his treks across the Andes, his voyages to the North and South Poles.

All his expeditions had the same goal: the discovery of cryptids, strange creatures whose existence has been mentioned, suspected, talked about in hushed whispers—but never truly confirmed by science. Creatures such as Bigfoot, the Loch Ness Monster, or the Atlantic Sea Serpent. Cryptids were Harold Mews's obsession, and they had become Annie's, too.

So, despite her parents' protests, Annie packed her bags, prepared the hot-air balloon, and took to the skies.

She was getting
close now, and she
saw that she was not the only one drawn to
the contest. She had a bird's-eye view of the road
leading into Bucky Cove; it was lined with hundreds
of vehicles, all approaching the small town.

And it wasn't just cars and trucks! All manner
of adventurers in all manner of vehicles were drawn
to the contest:

Another hot-air balloon, far in the distance.

A zeppelin, high above her.

An old biplane zooming past her, sputtering
and coughing.

Below her, a man in a hang glider swooping
and diving.

It would be quite the contest indeed. But Annie
had a leg up. She had studied cryptids. She knew
where to look and she knew—

Annie's thoughts were interrupted by a high-
pitched howl. Annie gripped the side of the basket
and spun.

It was a jet! Futuristic and fast. And it was
rocketing toward her . . .

"Oh, bananas!"
Annie shrieked as she
furiously adjusted the heat and jerked the
propeller.

"C'mon, c'mon . . ." Annie said, eyeing the
fast-approaching jet.

With a shrill shriek, the jet blasted past her.
Annie caught a quick glimpse of the pilot: a bug-
eyed woman with bright pink hair interrupted by
a white lightning-bolt-shaped streak. Across the
side of the jet were the words GRIMLOCK GLIDER. The
Grimlock Glider—shiny and silver, with upturned
wings and purple lines—looked like something out

of the old science-fiction magazines Annie loved
to read.

"Watch it, ya flying jerk!" Annie shouted.

The jet left a hot trail in its wake, causing an
updraft that rocked and tossed Annie's balloon.
Next came the downdraft, which forced the
balloon toward the ground. Annie cranked the
propane heater, but the air currents were too
strong. The balloon was out of control and sinking
fast.

Annie groaned as she desperately jerked the
propeller back and forth. *This adventure is off to a
fantastic start . . .*

Annie peeked over the side of the basket. The
ground beneath her was growing larger and larger
as she spiraled down faster and faster . . .

Chapter Two

The Contest

Mere feet above the road and just seconds before crashing, Annie flung the propeller lever and the balloon swooped back up, catching a wind current.

Annie may have avoided becoming a splattered splotch on the road, but she wasn't out of the woods yet—in fact, she was heading straight *into* the woods! The balloon was careening toward a small grouping of trees. She needed to get the balloon higher.

She spun the gear on the propane heater, giving it as much gas as it could handle.

Annie looked up. *Incoming tree!*

There was a loud *CRACK!* and then a *WHOOSH!* as the basket clipped the treetops. A leaf with a big bug on it flew into Annie's mouth and—*Yechh!*—she spit it out.

A long plastic banner was strung across the Main Street entrance to Bucky Cove. It read HAROLD MEWS WELCOMES THE WORLD'S GREATEST ADVENTURERS!

With a *rip,* Annie tore right through the banner. The plastic wrapped around her face so that she couldn't see.

"Bananas!" Annie exclaimed.

Thankfully, the wind ripped the banner away—just in time for Annie to see that she was on a collision course with a tall brick chimney poking out of the top of a cute old house.

"Double bananas!" she screamed. She threw the propeller lever again and sent the balloon swinging to the side. The basket scraped against the side of the house. A very round old woman with blue hair in white curlers stuck her fist out the window and called Annie all sorts of names.

"I'm really sorry!" Annie cried out as she swept past.

Annie and her balloon continued spinning and spiraling down Main Street. Annie deftly dodged awnings and trees and flagpoles and TV antennas and satellite dishes and weather vanes and everything else.

Annie squeaked. *Higher! I need to get higher!*

Then—oh no!—Annie spotted electrical lines up ahead, near the Mews mansion. Those would put a very quick, very shocking end to her adventure.

Lower, lower! I need to get lower!

Annie dropped the heat and threw open the vent, forcing the balloon to plummet downward. A rough landing was better than being barbecued!

The balloon slammed into the ground, and the basket crunched and scraped down the street, tossing Annie to the side. She quickly threw an armful of sandbags over the side. When they hit the ground, the whole contraption finally began to slow and then, at last, came to a stop.

Annie gulped in air and let out a huge sigh of relief. "Phew," she said, wiping her brow. "I hope no one saw that!"

And then she looked around.

Oh . . .

Man . . .

Annie had landed *right smack dab in the middle* of the massive crowd of fortune seekers that had gathered at the gates of the Mews mansion in anticipation of the contest announcement.

Everyone stared at Annie: gruff men and stern women, all with wide, judging eyes that said, "*Some adventurer you are! Be gone, young one!*"

Annie felt her face turn bright red. She waved her hand and smiled meekly. "Um, hi guys. I'm—

ah—I'm here for the contest?"

Thankfully, Annie's embarrassment was short-lived. The gate to the Mews mansion was opening! A hush fell over the crowd.

Is this him? Am I going to see him? Am I finally going to meet my hero?

A figure stepped out from behind the mansion gate. Annie frowned. No, it was not Mews. It was a man with the strict appearance of a butler. The man unrolled a single scroll of paper and loudly hammered it into the mansion's wooden gate.

The huge crowd continued to gather at the gate, all of them clambering to see what the butler had posted. Annie, smaller than all of them, was able to sneak her way through the crowd.

She saw the scroll nailed to the gate. As she read the words, her face lit up.

REWARD
$1,000,000
For irrefutable proof of the
existence of FOUR cryptids.
Search the world and bring your proof to
Harold Mews to claim your reward.
The first to return with proof
will be named the winner!

Annie grinned. She was right! It *was* a cryptid hunt. More than that, it was a *race!*

Murmurs of excitement spread through the thick throng of adventurers. Annie heard the words on their tongues.

"Contest!"

"Cryptid!"

"Race!"

Finally, one of the adventurers called out, "What are we waiting for?! The contest has begun!"

Chapter Three

False Starts and Rough Beginnings

They were off!

Hundreds of adventurers leaped into action, setting off in hopes of finding proof of a cryptid, departing in balloons and boats and helicopters and gyrocopters and big cars and small cars and off-road vehicles and on-road vehicles—everything imaginable!

Annie had hoped to meet Mr. Mews, to talk with him about their mutual love of and belief in the strange creatures classified as cryptids. But to meet him she'd need to win the contest. Annie grinned. *No problemo!*

Annie cranked up the heat, and the balloon lifted into the air. Beneath her, she saw that some other contestants' journeys had already ended:

A bright red hang glider was lodged in a

tree, and its pilot was hanging upside down by a shoelace.

A hot-air balloon not unlike Annie's had landed on a roof and was deflating fast. The owner of the house was out front, swatting at it with a rake.

A woman stood on the side of the road, hands on her hips, looking at her motorcycle as clouds of smoke billowed out of it.

Annie wondered if the same villain—the

woman behind the control stick of the *Grimlock Glider*—had knocked these rivals out of the contest. Annie ignored the thought. *No time to feel sorry for the competition, I've got a contest to win!*

Soon, Annie was soaring past the sandy beaches of Bucky Cove and out over the sea. She inhaled the rich aroma of the Atlantic Ocean and smiled. The adventure had begun.

Annie was heading east to Scotland, in hopes of getting a glimpse—and a photograph—of the most legendary cryptid of them all: the Loch Ness Monster.

Seagulls flapped and squawked, confused at the small girl in the big balloon taking up their airspace. One doofy-looking gull landed on the balloon's ledge.

"Hey there," Annie said to the doofy seagull, smiling. "You coming for the ride?"

The seagull squawked.

"You sure?" Annie asked, laughing to herself. "You're more than welcome to join me!"

The seagull's head cocked to the side, and it looked down to the ocean below. In a flash it flapped its wings and soared away.

"Guess not." Annie shrugged.

A moment later, Annie saw the reason for the gull's sudden departure: There was a speedboat drifting in the water below. It was purple and black with sharp silver lines. Its markings looked to be of the same design as the ones on the jet that had sent Annie spiraling out of control.

Annie floated closer and closer. She saw the words GRIMLOCK GUNNER in bright white on the side—beside them, an image of a woman with bug eyes with pink and white hair.

Bananas! It is her!

Annie watched as the cockpit shifted and slid back, revealing the same woman who had piloted the jet.

"Hello there, girl," the pink-haired woman shouted up to Annie.

Annie scowled and shouted back, "I'm glad to see you down on the water. You shouldn't be allowed in the sky—you nearly killed me!"

The woman laughed—a high-pitched cackle, like a hyena's. "Only nearly? Then I failed."

Annie scowled. *Stupid pink-haired jerk.*

"I'm sorry to be the one to tell you," the pink-haired woman continued, "but that million dollars is mine."

"Well, *I'm* sorry to be the one to tell *you*," Annie shouted back, "but you're in a boat, and I'm up in the sky. So there isn't a whole lot you can do to stop me!"

The pink-haired woman smiled a thin, wicked grin. She leaned forward and pressed a button on the boat's control panel. Suddenly, the back of the boat began to transform. A metal section slid back, there was a mechanical hum, and something began to rise from inside the boat.

It looked an awful lot like a cannon.

"Blast!" Annie exclaimed.

"Sorry to burst your balloon, but I suspect your first adventure will be your last," the woman said, reaching down. She was reaching for something . . . pressing something . . .

Uh-oh.